ALIDA'S SONG

GARY PAULSEN

A Dell Yearling Book

Published by
Dell Yearling
an imprint of
Random House Children's Books
a division of Random House, Inc.
New York

Visit us on the Web! www.randomhouse.com/kids

Educators and librarians, for a variety of teaching tools, visit us at www.randomhouse.com/teachers

---

ISBN: 0-440-41474-1

Reprinted by arrangement with Delacorte Press

Printed in the United States of America

April 2001

10 9 8 7 6

OPM

Dedicated with all love
to my grandmother and her song

Homecoming

"So you came home to see your old grandma, did you?"

"Yes."

"And now you are grown."

"Yes."

"And in the army." She said it *aaarmiie,* in a teasing way.

"Yes. I . . ."

"And you are a man. . . ."

"I . . . think so. Maybe . . ."

She stopped speaking for a moment then and

smiled and clicked her false teeth and put a sugar lump to her coffee, held it until it had soaked through, then put it under her tongue and sucked on it while she studied him in silence.

He looked around the small house where she lived with another old woman, named Florence. The family had hired Florence, who was in her seventies, to take care of his grandmother, who was a little older. But Florence was always "poorly," or so his grandmother said, and in reality his grandmother wound up looking after Florence, cooking for her, cleaning up after her, and he thought that perhaps it was best that way. His grandmother always took care of people, as she had always taken care of him.

"Are you happy?" The question was so sudden it startled him, and he did what he had always done with her sudden questions. He shrugged.

"I guess so."

She knew instantly that it was a lie. "You don't like the army?"

He shook his head. "No. I hate it. It was a terrible mistake to enlist."

"It will soon be over," she said.

"In three years." His voice had the edge of a whine to it and he was disgusted with himself.

She nodded. "Three years will go by like that." She clapped her hands. "You'll see. Do you have a girlfriend?"

He was still thinking about the army and about how three years did not seem like such a short time to him. He shook his head. "No. I don't know anybody."

She sighed. "You must find a girl and get married. It is the best thing for you—for a man—to be married."

He said nothing. He did not meet any girls, he thought, not women but girls—except in the places soldiers went to drink and find women, not girls but women, but he did not go to those places and had not yet begun to drink as he one day would. He knew no girls but the wives of sergeants in his unit and they were already married. He could have said that. He could have said lots of things, but he kept silent.

"Are those your own teeth?" she asked.

He nodded and didn't tell her of the back tooth kicked out by another recruit in a barracks fight during basic training.

"Let me see."

He leaned forward and opened his mouth to show his teeth. How many times, how many hundreds of times, had she said softly, "Let me see," to one thing or another, a cut, a bruise, a magic trick? And now, in that one act, he was no longer the man he thought he might be but was carried back to when he was just fourteen, just becoming a man.

Chapter One

At first the summer seemed to be much like other summers.

Many things were normal. Not good, but normal. He had nearly flunked the eighth grade, barely squeaking by, getting passed, he felt, because they didn't want him around the same rooms for another year, just as he had nearly flunked the seventh grade and the sixth grade before it, getting passed on because they did not want him around.

He still delivered newspapers in the morning

and still sold newspapers in the bars at night, hustling the drunks for extra dimes and quarters when they weren't looking.

Every night he went to the corner where Johnny delivered the papers wrapped in bundles and gathered forty papers. He went to the hospital first, working room to room until it was after nine. Then he went to the bars when the men and women would be too drunk to count their change very well.

"Come on, Charley, give the kid a buck. You're such a big spender. Give the kid a buck." And he—the kid—would smile in what he hoped was a winning way and look poor (not hard to do) and sometimes the drunk would listen to the woman and give him a buck. Considering he usually made only a nickel a paper in commission, a dollar represented twenty sales. With that and slipping extra change off the bar when they weren't looking, on a good night he might clear three or three and a half dollars—half a day's pay for a man working in a factory in those long-ago times.

His folks were still drunk. That hadn't changed. They lived in what he thought of as a grubby apartment. He didn't think of himself as living there and he spent as little time as possible in the apartment. He would go back there when it was late and they were so drunk they had passed out. He would rifle his mother's purse and his father's pants and get perhaps two more dollars. They never knew how much he had taken because they were always in blackouts; once he'd found a twenty-dollar bill in his father's pocket and they didn't even know it was gone. Then he'd take a quart of milk, a loaf of bread, a jar of peanut butter and another of grape jelly and head for the basement.

He had a place down there. The furnace was in a dark cubicle, near the coal bin. He was in charge of the furnace. In the winter the landlord paid him three dollars a week to feed coal to the stove hopper and to carry the clinkers out in a metal tub and scatter them on the driveway.

The furnace cubicle was his place, his own place, and he had found an old easy chair with the springs sticking through the cushion and dragged it back into the cubicle. There was a single bulb hanging from the ceiling on a twisted wire, a bulb with clear glass and a bare filament that was so bright it seemed like day when it was lit. He fashioned a shelf-table out of an old tabletop he'd found and would sit down there for hours, eating peanut butter and jelly sandwiches and drinking milk from the carton, trying to read (he read poorly) or making stick model airplanes. He relived the air war in the Second World War in the basement with the models—P-38s, B-17s, Corsairs, Zeros—that he painstakingly made of balsa wood and tissue paper. He hung them from the ceiling in the cubicle and when he needed room for new models he would take the old ones to the roof of the apartment building, sprinkle them with lighter fluid, light them and send them flying off into space to go down in flames.

This was done with great solemnity, and the curving down of the plane as it glided and crashed mimicked the crashing he'd seen in movies and newsreels of planes going down in combat. He always felt compassion for what it must have been like to die that way. He heard that some pilots carried pistols so they could shoot themselves if their plane caught on fire and they couldn't get out, and sometimes when he felt as if his life was impossible and he couldn't get out he wished he had a pistol. Not always, but sometimes.

He lived this way until it seemed to be all of his life. Usually he slept in the basement as well, though sometimes after his parents had passed out he would move back upstairs and sleep on the couch near the door—in case they awakened and he had to leave in a hurry. And he went upstairs to use the bathroom or shower.

His day was nearly always the same. He had

an old alarm clock with a little hammer that slapped back and forth against two bells so loudly that it could wake the dead. He rose at five, cleaned up, took his paper bag and walked the five blocks downtown to where Johnny brought the morning papers. He delivered subscription papers in the morning.

On the way he went by Torku's Bakery. They'd just be finishing the first run of hot rolls and he would go to the back door in the alley and knock softly and Mrs. Torku, who ran the ovens, would come and slip him three hot rolls. It had started because he'd walked through the alley one winter morning and the smell of baking bread had stopped him as dead as if he'd been hit with a hammer. He'd stood there salivating for a moment, then gone to the door to smell it better, and a large woman, not fat but large, had seen him there and given him some rolls. That was Mrs. Torku. "Those will take the chill out of the air," she said, and since then he'd stopped every morning to say hello and get hot rolls.

He would eat one immediately—the pleasure of the first hot roll was almost religious—and save the other two in his jacket pockets for later, just before school.

After the papers were delivered he would make his way to school, avoiding other children. He was almost terminally shy, especially with girls—doubly bad because he could not stop thinking of them—and had no real friends because of his home life and lack of social standing, and so he forgot most of what went on every day at school. Indeed, he often tried to forget it while it was happening, thinking, All right, this is happening now but I will forget it before tomorrow. He lived for weekends and holidays and summer, when he could be shed of all of it. Often he couldn't wait, but skipped school and either spent the day in the basement working on models, reading, or more often out in the woods near town hunting and fishing.

When school was done for the day he went to the Four Seasons Cafe, where he cleaned out the kitchen and trash and was paid a dollar and—usually, if he smiled right—he would get a hamburger and a Coke, which constituted his supper.

After that he would go to the bowling alley and set pins and then sell papers in the hospital and bars and back for the night to his basement hole, where he would work on the models or read.

Summer would come with its usual slow, dragging gait—the last week of school seemed to take a year. At last they'd give him his report card, which he'd throw away, along with a note from his teacher saying he could have done better, and he'd settle into the normal summer routine. This was largely the same as the winter's, except that he would try to find farm work for the day as well as the evening, and he'd go fishing down by the power dam every chance he could get for fish to sell in the bars.

This fourteenth summer started the same way and would have continued the same way except that in the first week after school was out he received a letter from his grandmother.

Dear One,

I am working now at the Nelson farm, cooking for two bachelor brothers named Gunnar and Olaf. They have fourteen cows and two hundred acres. They said they could use a boy for the summer. They said they would pay three dollars for each work day plus food and a bed on the porch. I have a quilt for you. You better come. It's a good job. Gunnar is coming down to Three Rivers next Tuesday for feed and will pick you up. I already told your mother you are coming. You better come so I can see you.

Love, Alida
Your Grandmother

He thought first of what he would miss by going to work at the Nelson farm with his grandmother for the summer. Fishing, work—he'd have to have somebody take his paper route and clean at the restaurant—and . . . that, he thought, was that. The rest he wouldn't miss. He certainly wouldn't miss his parents, the fighting and drinking.

He hadn't seen his grandmother since he was a small boy, and it would be nice to see her and in the end it was not as if he had much of a choice.

It was his grandmother, after all, and during the war while his mother worked in munitions factories in Chicago and lived a wild life he had stayed with his grandmother up in northern Minnesota, and he thought of her more as a mother than his own mother.

It would be like going home.

Chapter Two

Gunnar wore clean bib overalls and—in spite of the fact that it was June first—a denim coat with a checked flannel lining. He had a blue work shirt buttoned up to the collar, a straw hat with a green see-through visor, and plain glasses so thick his eyes expanded when he looked directly at the boy.

"You are ready?" He had a cleft palate, a birth defect in the roof of his mouth, and spoke in stilted English—although later the boy would hear him swear with great depth and beautiful fluency in Norwegian when a workhorse stepped on his foot. Because of the birth defect Gunnar's words seemed to hum and sounded musical. "Uuuuuurrrrrreedddy?"

The boy had been packed and ready for three days.

Gunnar was driving an old pickup—a 1938 Ford—that looked as if somebody had taken a sledgehammer and dented every square inch of the body. The windshield was in two pieces, with a brace down the middle, and the glass on the passenger side was broken out.

The boy put into the back of the truck a cardboard box containing some spare clothing, a model of a B-25 still in the box and a science fiction novel by Edgar Rice Burroughs called *The Chessmen of Mars*. He nestled the box into the corner of the bed behind the cab so it wouldn't blow away and began to climb into the passenger seat.

"Do you drive in town?" Gunnar stood by the

front of the truck and spoke through the broken windshield to the boy.

It was a loaded question. He was not old enough to drive legally, but he had worked on farms for two years now in the summer and had driven tractors and farm trucks and knew how to shift and drive. He also secretly drove the family car—a 1951 Chevy coupe—around town at night when his parents were passed out. He had to put a pillow on the seat to see out of the windshield, but he would drive past Irene Peterson's darkened house with his window open and his elbow propped up and fantasize about picking her up and taking her to the drive-in movie.

He shrugged. "Yes. I guess so."

"Good. You drive then. I am not so good at town driving. There are too many cars and too many signs. You have to think of everything." Gunnar went to the passenger side and motioned the boy to slide over behind the wheel. "I do not like to think of everything."

Well, the boy thought, I hope we don't meet a cop. He turned the key on, slid the floor gear-shift into neutral and mashed the starter switch on the floor next to the accelerator pedal. The truck ground over four times and just when it seemed on the edge of dying completely Gunnar pulled the choke out and the engine started with a belch of blue smoke. There was a hole in the muffler right below the floorboards—which were literally old boards and had holes here and there—and the noise and smoke came up into the cab.

"You need to choke her," Gunnar said. "Every time you start her."

The boy pushed the clutch down and put the truck in gear. "Where are we going? I don't know where your farm is."

"We are going to Grant first. Do you know where Grant is?"

The boy nodded. It was a small town—very small, with perhaps forty people—about twenty-five miles north of Three Rivers. He let the clutch out as he pushed his foot down on the gas, and the truck started to move.

He was still accelerating at the corner, where he turned onto Eighth Street, which went to the highway that led north of town to Grant. It was straight through except that there was a signal about halfway to the highway—three blocks down—and as they approached the signal the light turned red and the boy put his foot on the brake pedal.

It slammed to the floorboards without stopping. He pumped it as fast as he could but with no result. It just kept bouncing off the floor. "There are no brakes!" he shouted.

Gunnar nodded. "That is a thing I forgot to tell you. The brakes do not work. It had a set of cables to operate the brakes but a cable broke."

"But . . ." It was too late to say more. They were at the light and the boy looked right and left, saw cars coming—and a semitrailer—and he weaved left, then right, closing his eyes, and when he opened them the pickup was through the intersection.

"I—"

"Drivers will move," Gunnar said, "if they have to move. They do not want to hit us."

The boy slowed the truck to little more than a crawl along the side of the road. "You drove all the way down here like this?"

Gunnar nodded. "The cable broke as I was leaving. We needed the feed for the pigs and geese. I had to come."

"But we can't drive like this."

Gunnar shrugged and filled his lower lip with snuff. "If the truck could get to Three Rivers like this it can get home like this. What is the difference?"

"But how can we stop?"

"We will stop the engine. The truck will stop if the engine stops. It is possible if we drive at a slow rate of speed." He smiled, teeth stained by snuff. "But I think we could go faster than this."

The boy hesitated, then thought how much he liked to drive and that this was, at least, driving. He looked to the rear—there were no rearview mirrors—and pulled back onto the road and increased speed. The speedometer didn't work either so he accelerated to what he thought might be forty miles an hour—he saw Gunnar tighten up—and he held that as they drove north up the small, two-lane highway bordered on both sides by thick forest.

In three quarters of an hour—Gunnar didn't speak the whole time—he saw the grain-elevator tower of Grant, about a mile before town, and Gunnar pointed ahead at a gravel road heading off left, to the west. "Go that way."

The boy took his foot off the gas and the transmission slowed the truck well before the turn. Once on the road he brought the speed back up to thirty, or what felt like thirty. "How far is it?"

"We must go this way seven farms and then north for three farms. The third farm is ours.

You will see a white house and a red barn with a brick silo and that will tell you it is our farm."

The boy nodded and started counting farms. There were more open fields now, cleared land around each farm, and while the buildings were often back in trees they were easy to see.

Every single farm had a white house and red barn and brick silo. Nevertheless the boy counted farms and when he reached seven he saw a smaller road leading north. He slowed and turned in the fading light and after four more miles Gunnar said, "There. On the right. That is our farm."

At an old mailbox the boy turned right and drove up a quarter-mile driveway to the farm-yard. It was nearly dark—and just as well, for the boy found later that the headlights didn't work any better than the brakes—but he could see that the farm looked neat and clean. A black-and-white cross-collie dog came out to meet the truck, its tail wagging so hard it nearly fell over, and when the truck ground to a stop in the yard the boy looked at the house and saw his grandmother coming from the door.

She was tiny. He always remembered her as large—not fat, but she was large in his mind, mostly because he had lived with her when he was very young and remembered her from then. It surprised him to see how small she really was, and as short as he was, as he got out of the truck and went to where she stood at the gate with her hands wrapped in her apron, a bit of flour on her cheek and some dusted in her hair, he found himself looking down on her.

"Hello, Grandma," he said.

She looked at him for a long time—half a minute—without speaking and then she smiled, first her eyes and then her mouth, and said, "It's good to see you. Come and eat. You look like you need food."

Chapter Three

He was dreaming about the bowling alley. He was setting pins, double alley, working in the rhythm as he swung back and forth between alleys: pick up the ball and flip it into the ball return, grab three pins in each hand, slap them into the pin machine, swing to the next alley. It was league bowling and he was making eleven cents a line—four more cents than the seven cents he made for weekend bowling—and men were jamming dollar tips into the ball holes on their balls. He had money stuffed in all his pockets and still they sent more, dollar bills flying out of the balls when he picked them up . . .

"You must wake up now." Somebody was shaking him. "It is time to get up."

He opened his eyes and saw his grandmother backlit by a Coleman lantern in the kitchen. He was on a bed on the screened-in porch. It was still pitch dark. "Up? Now? What time is it?"

"Time to get up," she said, and left him there, and he soon heard the sound of stove lids scraping and paper rustling as she lit a fire in the kitchen stove.

It can't be, he thought. It's still hours before dawn. He rolled over and closed his eyes and tried to find the dream again—so *much* money—but no sooner had his eyes closed than she was back. "Now." Her voice firm but not sharp. "There are chores to do."

"All right. I'm awake." He sat up and realized that he needed to go to the bathroom. She had fed him an enormous supper—meat and potatoes and corn and a second meat and apple pie—and it now made demands on him. "Where's the bathroom?" he called from the porch to the kitchen.

"There's an outhouse. Out the door and to the left. Mind the geese, they should be waking up about now."

"Geese?" he asked, but she didn't hear him and the urgency was too great. He ran for the door in his underwear and to the outhouse, tripping on the step up into the small building. When he was done he looked for toilet paper and could find nothing but what felt like an old catalog. He tore pages from it and finished and opened the door to head back to the house.

Halfway there, still a good twenty paces from the door, he was attacked by—he found later—twenty-one geese. It was so abrupt and so unexpected—the geese were gray and were hardly visible until they were on him—that he thought it was some kind of monster.

Hissing and flapping their wings, they hit him

from the back and side at the same time. He swung and hit something soft, which fell down and away, but eight or ten others were on him and he yelled—he remembered yelling and swearing—and then something exploded against the back of his head and he was on his hands and knees and then it hit again, this time against the side of his head, and he went down.

He had a vague image of somebody who looked a lot like his grandmother towering over him, swinging a broom left and right, and then there was a bright flash of color and he saw nothing.

He awakened slowly, his head pounding. He was back in his cot on the porch and his grandmother was standing over him. To her rear were Gunnar and Olaf. They all looked concerned.

"What happened?" the boy asked. "I was just coming back from the outhouse . . ."

"It was the geese," Olaf said. He had a low

voice, soft, and seemed many years older than Gunnar. "They don't like strangers."

"Don't like? They almost killed me."

"It's their wings," his grandmother said. "They have a trigger in their wings. They hit with the end of the first joint so hard they can drop a dog. It looks like they hit you at least three times."

He raised his hand and felt three large lumps forming. The pain was sharp but subsiding and he sat up. He was still in his underwear and he pulled his pants on. It felt nice to have his grandmother worry over him but he was embarrassed to act like a baby in front of the two old men.

It was still dark outside, the only light coming from the Coleman lantern in the kitchen. The stove was hot and the air was cool enough that it felt good to go into the warm kitchen before lacing his boots. There was coffee boiling. It was straight pot-boiled coffee and his grandmother took some eggshells off the warming oven and threw them into the pot on top of the grounds. Then she dumped in a ladle of cold water from the water bucket on the counter—the farm, it turned out, had no electricity or running water—and handed each of them a clean cup. She poured coffee for them as they stood by the stove.

The boy put three heaping teaspoons of sugar from the bowl on the kitchen table into the cup and stirred it and drank carefully. It was very hot, and very sweet—the way he liked it—but his whole head felt sensitive to pain and the burn on his lips seemed to add to the ache in his skull.

"Why did you put eggshells into the coffee?" he asked. The two men sat at the table and drank their coffee so quickly that he thought they must have throats made of iron. They seemed to be swallowing steam.

"It takes the bitterness away," she answered. "Can't you taste that the bite is gone?"

"With so much sugar there wouldn't ever *be* a bite." Gunnar hummed the words and held his cup out for more coffee. The boy's grandmother filled both men's cups and put a plate of cookies on the table next to a plate of rolls. Near the rolls was a bowl full of butter and a quart jar of jam.

"Have something," she said. "Before work starts—just to get you to breakfast."

The boy took a roll—thinking of the bakery rolls he was given each morning on his paper route—and used a knife with a wooden handle to cover it with butter and jam. When he put the knife down Gunnar picked it up and split a roll and added butter and jam and when he was done Olaf did the same and the three of them ate until all the rolls—there must have been a dozen—were gone.

Then the men dipped cookies in their coffee—the boy copied them—until the cookies were gone.

"Well," Gunnar said, standing. "The cows are probably busting."

He made for the door and Olaf followed him. The boy didn't know what to do at first but his grandmother was standing by the stove. She was sifting flour for bread and had flour in her hair—he would never remember her for the rest of his life without flour in her hair—and she nodded toward the door. "Go with them."

He had worked farms the previous two summers and knew how hard the labor was but it was different here and he saw the difference as soon as he got to the barn.

The sun was just showing light in the east over a long green flat of pasture that led down to a small stream a hundred yards from the barn. Mist came up from the stream and layered the grass. The cows—huge black-and-white ghosts—were making their way toward the barn through the mist as if walking on air.

Both Olaf and Gunnar stood by the back door of the barn watching.

"Never," Gunnar whispered as the boy came up. "Never seen nothing so pretty, have you?"

The boy stopped and Olaf put a hand on his shoulder. Normally he hated to be touched. At one farm he'd worked at part of the previous summer a man had whipped him for doing something wrong; once when he was smaller a man had struck him. He started to back away from Olaf. But this was different in some way, as if Olaf were touching a dog or a friend, and the boy found he didn't mind.

"See how they come?" Olaf said. "It's so old—cows have been coming to barns since before . . . before everything."

"Did they when you were young?" Olaf and Gunnar seemed ancient to the boy—in their sixties at least, maybe older than his grandmother.

"Always. Back in Norway they came this way, and before that. I have pictures in the house to show you from then."

"You talk too much," Gunnar said softly. "Just watch—you don't have to talk."

And so they stood and watched the cows plod

along toward them, stood and wasted five or six minutes, and it was the first time working on a farm the boy had ever seen such a thing. Standing when there was work to be done.

"Here, here . . ." Olaf spoke softly as the cows moved into the barn on their own. "Just here, girls, come on in."

The cows found their own stanchions and Olaf and Gunnar started milking. They milked by hand and did not ask or tell the boy to help. He knew how to milk, knew how to squeeze to get the milk to start, but he was not good at it and he also knew that if a cow was milked wrong it made her bind up and not lower the milk.

The boy hated to stand and do nothing and he found a shovel at the end of the barn and cleaned the gutters while Olaf and Gunnar milked.

When they had milked five or six cows Gunnar motioned to the boy with his chin. "Come turn the separator."

At the end of the barn there was a cool room,

a room with a water tank in the end of it to store the milk cans, with water filtering through from a windmill and tank over the granary.

In the center of the cool room was a hand-cranked milk separator with a large stainless-steel tub on top to pour the milk in and two spouts coming out to two buckets on the floor—one for milk and one for the cream that was separated from the milk.

The separator worked by centrifugal force, caused by spinning some disks in an enclosed chamber while milk dripped down on them from the bowl on top. The spin was furnished by a hand crank and the boy started cranking it, faster and faster until the disks spun with a high whine.

Once it came up to speed it was not hard to keep going and he had time to watch two cats that came into the barn trying to catch the milk from the spout. He would have stopped them but they were doing it when Gunnar came in and he didn't stop them so the boy assumed it was all right.

One of them was experienced and leaned out over the bucket and deftly lapped from the stream as it came down.

The other, the boy decided, had something wrong with his head, or was just stupid. He would look at the falling stream, open his mouth wide and stick his whole head under the downpour. It splashed in his eyes, some in his mouth, back in his ears and down his neck, and he would jump back as if he'd been scalded and would spit and then stop, smell himself, lick it all off and start over.

All in all it made the separating go fast—like having entertainment—and chores were over before the boy knew it.

They put the milk cans on a concrete ledge in the cool tank—twice a week the milk truck came for the milk and cream—and walked back up to the house for breakfast.

On the way they passed the geese. The instant the birds saw the boy they all raised their wings and lowered their heads and hissed and came at him.

For a second he started to run but Olaf swore at them in Norwegian and they stopped and lowered their wings and moved off—although they would look back at the boy and hiss until he was at the door of the house and inside.

It was not, he thought, over yet. If they caught him alone it would be like when the street kids tried to catch him and beat him up and take the money he'd made selling papers.

He'd have to fight the geese.

Chapter Four

They had been working only two hours—cows in from the pasture, milked, and let back out to the pasture—but the boy found he was starving when they went in for breakfast.

His grandmother had made pancakes, a huge stack of them, and there was birch syrup and more coffee and rolls with raspberry jelly and doughnuts and strips of fried meat he found later was venison and fresh milk and fresh bread to put in the milk and sprinkle sugar on and eat for dessert when breakfast was at last done.

The boy did not think he could move but Olaf grunted and stood and looked at his grandmother and then back to the boy and said, "Come with me to check for mustard."

Which made no sense at all, but he followed. Olaf put on a denim, plaid-flannel-lined jacket, though it was warm enough for the boy to wear only a T-shirt, and they left the house and headed back around the front yard.

The house was two-story, frame, old and in slight need of paint, surrounded close in by a small picket fence that was also in need of paint. The grass in the yard needed mowing as well—or would in a week—and the whole of it, the barn, granaries, toolshed and house, lay in the exact center of four forty-acre fields. Across the road from the house, close but set slightly apart, lay another forty-acre plot, and Olaf and Gunnar had all five forties planted. Two were in oats and barley, one was in wheat and two were in corn. They were all well up—the corn halfway to the knee—and all looked clean and well tended.

"We'll do the corn," Olaf said, heading for the two fields of corn. "Mind you step only in the rows."

The boy was still confused but he followed along as Olaf entered the cornfield and walked along and when he came to a weed he pulled it up by the roots.

"We get the mustard now, before it goes to seed and makes new plants and soon there are no more weeds."

From working on other farms the boy knew of the mustard weed—so called because it had a small flower that was the yellow of mustard. It was everywhere and strangled other plants out, ruining crops. Most farmers used a tractor and tanks of fluid and sprayed to kill it.

"You're going to *pick* all the mustard?" he asked.

Olaf smiled. "We always do. There are times

when not so many other things need to be done and it is nice to walk through the fields of a morning and pull weeds. Here, try it. You take those two rows and I'll take these."

The boy started down the rows and when he looked he saw that there weren't very many weeds in the field. A hundred or so in the whole forty-acre stand of corn.

"There are hardly any of them. How long have you been doing this, picking the weeds?"

Olaf, two rows off, smiled. "My whole life. My grandfather picked them, my father picked them and I'm picking them. They've never had a chance to get a start."

They moved through the field pulling weeds. In the middle of the morning his grandmother came out to the edge of the corn with a large cream bucket with a lid and called to them.

"Forenoon lunch." Olaf looked at the sun. "I didn't think it was that late."

They walked carefully through the corn and sat in the grass at the edge of the field, where his grandmother spread a tablecloth. The cloth was made of sewn-together feed sacks with pictures of chickens and sheep on them, along with a large red diamond and the name RED DIAMOND FEED circled around the sheep and chickens protecting them.

The boy sat at one end and Olaf at the other and his grandmother in the middle. She put out two plates with a fresh loaf of bread and cut pieces of venison and a bowl of butter and a quart jar filled with hot coffee wrapped in another feed sack to keep it warm. There were two cups and sugar in a Ball pint canning jar, rhubarb sauce in another, a jar of chokecherry jelly and salt in another jar.

The boy reached for the bread but Olaf took a breath and said:

"I would like to thank God for the meal."

The boy pulled his hands back and put them together and Olaf took another breath and said:

"Thank you, God, for this food."

The boy waited but that comprised the whole

prayer. Olaf reached for bread and meat and the boy made a sandwich and they ate in silence. His grandmother did not eat. The boy realized then that he almost never saw her eat, could not remember her eating.

"Grandma," he said. "You never eat."

Olaf smiled and said nothing for a moment and his grandmother nodded. "I get here and there. I eat when I cook, bits and pieces. Food finds my mouth."

"But I've never seen you sit down and eat a meal."

She shook her head and waved a hand as if shooing a fly. "It's because I cook."

"This is so?" Olaf stopped chewing. "You never sit to eat?"

"It's not a thing to think about." The boy was surprised to see she was blushing. "I'm always busy cooking. It is not something to mind."

"No," Olaf said. "It is there you are wrong. It is only right that you sit to eat. Tonight we will cook for you for a change."

"But you hired me to cook. That is why I am here."

Olaf nodded. "That is true. But we did not hire your whole life. There must be a little easing here and there. Tonight we will cook and the boy"—he smiled—"can clean up after us. Is that all right?"

It took a moment for the boy to realize that Olaf was asking him, not her. Rarely did adults ask for his approval and it surprised him. "Sure."

"There it is, then," Olaf said, standing. "We will work the day out and then stop before dark to cook." He walked off into the field, pulling at mustard plants while the boy took a bite of sandwich and followed him, grabbing weeds, thinking that of all the places he had worked, and all the work he had done, this was perhaps the strangest place of all.

Chapter Five

The boy sometimes had soft dreams. He had hard dreams more often—about people not liking him, about having everybody in school staring at him, about his father drunk throwing him through a kitchen window—but sometimes he had soft dreams and usually when he dreamed softly it was of his grandmother.

She had raised him for most of his young years and even when he wasn't with her in some way she had continued to raise him because he thought of her often, thought of what she would say or do if she saw him doing something wrong. Not of what his mother would say or what his father would say but what his grandmother would say.

Once when he was very small, maybe three, he had awakened in the night with terrible pain in his knees. No matter what he did, bend them, straighten them—no matter, the pain was there, aching, pushing from the joint both up and down in his legs, and he had cried. His grandmother had come into the room. He could not remember even where it had happened or for sure when, but his grandmother had come into the darkened room and sat on the edge of the bed and put her hands on his knees and pushed down gently, just the softest pressure, and had sung a quiet song in Norwegian and the pain had gone away.

He dreamed of that now, as he worked in the field until lunch, letting his mind go to pleasant things, watching Olaf out ahead of him, listening to Olaf humming. Sometimes Olaf broke into

Norwegian, but usually he hummed, and the boy felt relaxed as the morning sun hit his back and he thought, I have been here only half a full day and it seems as if I've never been anyplace else.

They went to the house for lunch—which they called dinner, as opposed to the evening meal, which they called supper. The noon dinner was a meal that would have foundered many.

There were three kinds of meat—venison, pork and beef, as well as blood sausage, which the boy ate before he knew what it was, and liked it, and couldn't eat after he knew. There were mashed potatoes, fresh-baked bread with buttered crust, a bowl of freshly churned butter sprinkled with coarse salt, rhubarb preserves in sauce, canned peaches, new-baked apple pie and, for the boy, fresh chilled whole milk from the milk house on the barn. There were also coffee and grape juice with water and sugar added and small green onions to dip in a bowl of salt with each bite.

They ate for a full hour and the boy did not

see how in any way he could *ever* eat again, let alone that day. He could hardly walk when they stumbled out into the sun and back out to the fields.

Gunnar had hooked the team of horses to a cultivator and was working the soil on the other side of the field, which took out most of the weeds between the rows but not the mustard growing in with the corn.

The horses had done it many times and knew what to do and walked evenly without stepping on the corn while the chisel teeth scraped along and turned the spaces in the middle into new earth, thick and black against the green.

It was not hard work but they kept at it steadily all that afternoon, and well before dark Gunnar stopped the horses at the end of the field and Olaf looked at the sun and saw the boy back in the corn and said, "Come, it's time for evening chores."

They made their way to the barn and Gunnar called the cows—they were closer in now, drinking water in the tank by the barn—and they milked as they had in the morning, the boy cranking the separator and the men pulling the milk.

There was a difference now, however. They whistled and sang and hummed with the sounds of the cows and the whine of the separator but now and then they would stop and Olaf would say:

"We should have potato sausage. She would like potato sausage. With melted butter."

"And milked potatoes," Gunnar would answer. "They go well with potato sausage."

"We have those plums we picked and canned last year before she came," Olaf added. "They taste like summer."

"And kraut from the crock. I'll rinse it to take the salt out." Gunnar poured the last of the milk into the separator. "And gunpowder biscuits and after we eat you can fiddle and I will slap bones and the boy and I might play *krokono*—"

"What's *krokono*?" the boy asked.

"It's a game," Gunnar said, "that you play on your lap by snapping doughnuts at each other."

"Oh." And the boy thought if he didn't want to tell me he should have just said so—he didn't have to make up silliness—but the moment passed and they went to the house carrying the dirty buckets and separator parts.

His grandmother was in the kitchen when they came in and she took the buckets to the sink but Olaf stopped her.

"No. You must sit and watch. Or you can go and read. I have three books in the front room which have never been read and need reading. The boy will clean and we will cook now."

And he would have it no other way.

Chapter Six

They went well into night and all of it was new to the boy. Though he loved his grandmother—and he frequently thought of it that way, that of all the adult people in his life he loved only his grandmother—he came from a different world. He was from a city—or at least a large town—where they had electricity and radio and television (though it was new then and not everybody had it and there were only two channels, which often had snowy pictures, and all he had ever seen was blurred) and traffic and other people.

Here it was quiet and with no danger other than the geese—which came at the boy as he walked from the barn to the house with empty buckets and by god, he thought, *that* gander wouldn't try it again, having taken a bucket across the side of the head so hard it staggered away with one wing down and flapping—and no electricity and no radio. Not even lights. It was all different, all new to him.

In the kitchen there was the Coleman lantern hanging from the ceiling, which hissed and gave off a flat white light, but this evening Olaf did not fire up the lantern. Instead he used oil lamps. He lit two of them in the kitchen and adjusted the wicks to give off a soft yellow light and the boy's grandmother at last relented and stopped working, although she did not leave the kitchen but sat in the corner by the oil lamp and crocheted while she watched the men cook.

They filled a large pan with hot water from the reservoir on the cookstove, which stood by the kitchen sink and hand pump, and as they dirtied a pan or dish they would throw it to the boy at the sink and he would wash it and dry it and hand it back and they would dirty it again.

Olaf brought out casings packed in salt from a jar under the sink. They looked like pale dead snakes and the boy could not see what they would be used for until Olaf rinsed them in fresh cold water to take the salt off and cut them in four-foot pieces.

"Hog guts," Olaf said to the boy. "They make the best casings."

Not for me they don't, the boy thought. But he remained quiet and watched Olaf and Gunnar peel potatoes and process them in a hand grinder, then mix them with raw ground-up venison and a little salt.

Gunnar put a large pot of water on the stove and added pitch pine to the fire under the burners. This had the same effect as pouring gas on a fire and the stove became nearly red hot. It was summer and though the evening was cooler than the day it wasn't *that* cool and soon the kitchen was sweltering. Olaf and Gunnar both took off their shirts and the boy was surprised to see they were wearing long underwear. They kept their bib overalls on and pulled the shoulder straps back up, and with a word of apology to the boy's grandmother at having to "show their unders," went back to work.

The boy was wearing a T-shirt and decided it would be better not to go down to skin so he kept the shirt on and poured sweat over the sink.

The men cooked like fiends, all the while keeping up a steady banter.

"I had an uncle in the old country," Olaf said, "who said he used a shotgun barrel for stuffing sausage and just shot it in there but I don't believe him. He told me he'd seen a mermaid too but that she didn't have scales, only skin."

"Everybody knows a mermaid has scales,"

Gunnar cut in, his voice singsonging. "Otherwise they wouldn't be half fish."

Olaf had an old cow horn with the end cut off and tapered with carved rings for the casing to grip. He pushed one end of the casing over the horn and began stuffing the casing full of ground potatoes and meat, working the mixture down until the casing was full—not packed tightly but snug. He did four feet, then another piece, then another until there were twelve full feet of stuffed sausage.

This he coiled into loops and put in the boiling water on the stove.

In the meantime Gunnar had been working with flour and water and made dough for rolls—which he and Olaf called biscuits—and he let them rise near the heat of the stove before putting them in the oven.

While the rolls were rising Gunnar put sliced potatoes with milk over them in a large pan in the oven to bake, and forty minutes later it was pitch dark outside and the meal was on the table.

Olaf and Gunnar put their shirts back on, the boy set the table around the food and Olaf said, "A minute."

He put a pan on the stove with a full pound of butter in it and when the butter was melted he poured it into four bowls on the table, sprinkled salt and pepper on the top and they sat to eat.

"Thank you, God," Olaf said, "for this food."

"It is in this way," Gunnar said, "that you eat. You take a foot or so of sausage on your plate, cut a piece off the end, dip it in melted butter and swallow it."

The boy had hesitated about the sausage, especially when he saw it come out of the boiling water like a fat gray snake. But a piece cut on the plate didn't look so bad—and he knew all the horror stories about hot dogs and bologna—and once he tasted it, the potatoes and meat and melted butter completely changed his mind and to his utter amazement he found that in spite of the large lunch he was famished.

"Alida, you will sit at the end of the table,"

Olaf had told her, "and you only have to point at what you want."

"I cannot speak?"

Olaf smiled. "Only to ask."

So she sat and they fed her and they ate too—the boy ate a full four feet of sausage—and had plums and rolls and milk potatoes and fresh honey from a nearby bee farm for the rolls and when they were done the boy did the dishes while Olaf and Gunnar smoked pipes and when the dishes were done they took the lamps and carried them into the sitting room.

The boy had seen it in the morning but not been in it and found a room out of the late 1800s. There was old wood furniture and flower-papered walls and a bookshelf with three—just three—books on it, the three Olaf had told the boy's grandmother "needed reading." The windows had lacy curtains and every corner had shelves filled with small pictures and knick-knacks. There was a long couch and an easy chair with soft cushions, tables at either end of the couch and a low coffee table.

The boy's grandmother sat quietly at one end of the couch, her crochet needle flying, and Olaf sat at the other smoking his pipe. Gunnar went to a bookcase at the side and came back with a board about three feet square with net pockets in the four corners.

"Get a kitchen chair," he told the boy, "and bring it in here."

The boy did as he was told and Gunnar had him place it opposite the easy chair. "Sit."

The boy sat and Gunnar sat and put the playing board on their knees so that it was flat between them. He then took out a small cloth bag and dumped what appeared to be two dozen small wooden doughnuts on the board. Half of them were black, half red.

"Here, this red one with the black mark is your shooter. See the pockets at the corners? You must snap your shooter with your finger and hit my black doughnuts with your shooter and knock them in the pockets."

"Like pool," the boy said. "Or sort of."

Gunnar nodded. "Just so. A kind of billiards except that it is called *krokono*. Each time you make one of my doughnuts you get another shot. If you miss I will take a shot. Do not," he said, smiling, "miss."

The boy snapped and missed his first shot and watched Gunnar clean the table.

"You're good at this," the boy said, and Gunnar smiled.

"I have hard fingers. It makes it easy to aim before I snap. Let us play again."

This time the boy was careful and got two of Gunnar's doughnuts before he lost. The third game he was better still but he knew that if he played his whole life he would not beat Gunnar. Still it was fun and the boy got into the game and even when his snapping finger was in agony—the doughnuts were heavy and hurt when snapped—he did not want to quit and would not have quit except that Olaf left the room and came back in a minute with a violin case.

The boy's grandmother smiled and put her crocheting down. "Music," she said. "I do like music."

Gunnar put the doughnuts back in the bag and left the room and came back with two polished pieces of rib bone, which he held between his fingers and clicked against his knee as he sat in the chair.

"Something fast first," Gunnar said, looking to Olaf, "to wake us up."

Olaf nodded, tuned the violin for a moment, then broke into a fast melody with a chop to it. Gunnar picked it up, rapping the bones together against his knees with an almost hollow ringing sound, and the boy saw his grandmother's foot tapping and her fingers drumming on the arm of the couch, and Gunnar's eyes closed and he doubled the rhythm of the bones between the notes of the violin, and Olaf stood close to Gunnar so the music and *click-clack* of the bones went together, and soon the boy's foot was jumping as well as his arm and he was smiling and didn't know he was smiling.

The tune lasted five minutes and the men drank water—it was hot in the sitting room with the heat from the kitchen stove working into the small space—and then Olaf started another, slower melody and Gunnar muted the bones and slowed the rhythm to a gentle waltz and the boy was surprised to see his grandmother get up and come to him, holding out her hand.

"Come. We will dance."

He hesitated and then sighed. "I don't know how to dance."

She stopped. "How can that be? Everybody dances."

He didn't want to speak of it in front of Olaf and Gunnar but they kept playing and seemed not to hear and politely looked away. "I don't know any girls . . . nobody has taught me."

She smiled. "Then you shall learn."

"Here? Now?"

"Where better? You have your own music and your own teacher. Come, give me your hand and put your feet here, this way, then this way and this way . . ."

And she moved, pushing him to lead, turning him until he could turn himself, until he stopped tripping on his own feet and tromping on hers and he could feel the beat of the music and his feet sometimes were in the right place at the right time.

He did not know how long they danced. Olaf moved from one song to the next, Gunnar worked the bones and sometimes hummed in a soft birdlike voice with the violin, and the heat and work of the day seemed to evaporate with the music and when it was finally finished and he went to bed on the porch he knew only that it was dark and that he was wonderfully tired.

"The first Saturday is coming," his grandmother said as she blew out the lamp on the porch. "We will go to town then and see if the lessons took."

And he wanted to ask what she meant but his eyes closed on this first full day and no matter how hard he tried they would not come open again and he fell asleep with the sound of the bones and the violin in his ears and no memory of what she had said.

Chapter Seven

It was no way he had ever worked before.

Oh, the work was there. It was a farm and farms required work. The fields were all planted and for the most part weeded and cultivated but there were the chores to do and the barn to clean and the geese to evade and wood to chop and carry for the cookstove and the water to pump and the feed to mix for the pigs and calves in the pens next to the barn and lunches to eat and dinners to eat and suppers to eat and then more wood to split and more feed to carry and the picket fence to paint and more cows to milk and . . .

Sometimes it seemed the boy met himself coming around the corner of the barn with a bucket of feed or a forkful of manure.

But there was something else to this place, another way of looking at things he had never seen before.

One day he had gone with Gunnar and the workhorses to fix fence at the back of the pasture. He loved the horses. They were enormous—each probably over a ton—and so strong that Gunnar had used them to pull stumps out of the ground but they were very quiet and gentle.

This day Gunnar harnessed them and hitched them to a four-wheeled wagon. He threw fencing tools into the back and headed for the back pasture, where a windstorm had blown some trees across the wire and knocked it down, and the boy rode on the back of the wagon, letting his heels bounce along the grass, watching the dog trot and stop to smell gopher holes.

He was half dozing when he noticed a white rock sticking out of the ground. It was perhaps a foot across, nearly round—so smooth a shape that it caught his eye and kept him watching as they rode past. When they came to the other side of the rock he saw that it was a face, a woman's face carved in stone in the middle of the pasture.

"Gunnar," he said. "What's that?"

"What?"

"That rock. It looks just like a girl's head."

"That's Wilhelmina."

"Who is Wilhelmina?"

"A girl I used to know when I was young. Very young. As young as you."

"Who carved the rock?"

"I did."

The boy jumped off the wagon and stopped to look more closely at the carving. It was, he thought, elegant. He never used the word but it came to his mind now. He'd heard it in a movie once used to describe a beautiful woman and he thought the carving was that way—elegant. She had a fine straight nose and eyes that tilted up at the corners and a soft line of hair down the side, all carved and smoothed and polished so that the girl seemed almost alive, as if her head were pushing out of the ground and the rest of her were in the earth.

He squatted and looked more closely but could see no bad cuts, no flaws, just smooth white stone with a line here and there to suggest hair. A pretty girl, he thought. She was a very pretty girl and he was there, looking at her, when his eye saw another stone off a bit, thirty or forty yards, this one round and gray, almost too round, and he moved to it and saw it was the carved head of another girl. This one seemed very familiar in some way and he called to Gunnar again, "Who is this? It seems like I know her."

"You do. That is your grandmother Alida." Gunnar looked away. "When she was young."

And the boy could see it now, when he knew, could see her eyes and the shape of her head. Then he saw more. Standing there, he could see four, five . . . seven of them scattered around, all heads with faces looking across the grass.

"We have fence to do," Gunnar called, the words singing with his speech defect. *Weeavefuuuncctodo.* "Come now."

The boy trotted back to the wagon. "They were pretty." The word seemed wrong, too little. "Beautiful. They were beautiful."

"Thank you."

"Were they all girls you knew—like girl-friends?"

"Girls I saw, yes. Not all friends. Some of them never saw me. Did not look at me. Did not know me because of my . . . because."

"How many—how many carvings are there?"

"I do not know. Some of them I have forgotten and some of them are covered now. Each fall when harvest is done and before winter sets in I do a carving. Most of them are in stone, some are in wood back in the trees at the other end of the pasture."

They worked fence all day and when the chores were done that night the boy went out alone before dark and walked through the woods at the end of the pasture and saw them. Standing trees, faces carved and sometimes bodies, not whole bodies but an arm, a hand, the curve of a leg, always a face and the neck carved, in a pine tree or a poplar. He did not count them but there were many, over a dozen in the trees, and he did not know how many rocks and he walked through the ones in the trees and it was like being with people. He closed his eyes and could almost hear them talking, giggling, making girl sounds, the ones that made him so shy, and he felt bad at first for Gunnar, bad that he had never had a girlfriend, and then not so bad. Gunnar had many of them, all right here, all beautiful and graceful. Whenever he wanted to be with them he could walk out here and they would always be young and always be pretty.

There came a day when the boy was working in the yard, not going out in the fields. He always kept one eye on the geese. They had accepted him in their fashion—that is, they wouldn't attack him if they knew he was watching them. He had seen a story once in a *National Geographic* magazine about tigers in India that killed and ate people. The people thought the tigers wouldn't attack if they knew they were being watched so the people wore masks on the backs of their heads when they went into the forest to make the tigers believe they were being watched. The boy thought of doing the same thing with the geese but they seemed to have quieted—perhaps hitting the gander with the bucket had made a mark—and he was going into the barn to scrape out the gutters when he heard a strange whining sound coming from the milk room.

He stopped and listened and realized it was somebody humming and he opened the door to find Olaf standing by the separator. He had a Red Chief notebook and he was making marks on paper while he hummed.

"Hello," he said when the boy walked in. "I hope the sound did not bother you."

"No . . . not at all. What are you doing?"

"I'm writing some music. For your grandmother. See?" He held the notebook so the boy could see the page.

At the top in all capitals were the words:

ALIDA'S SONG

And down the page were squiggles and dots inside lines. The boy had seen musical notes in books in school but these were different. It was Olaf's private way and only he knew how to read it.

"How does it sound?" the boy asked.

"It's not done yet. I'll play it the first Saturday."

There it was again. This time the boy remembered his grandmother saying it when he went to bed at the end of the first day. "What does that mean, the first Saturday?"

Olaf smiled. "The first Saturday of every month we go to town. There is a dance. We play the music for the dance. It is this next Saturday. That is why I am working on the song. Next Saturday is a special day for your grandmother."

"What do you mean?"

"It is her anniversary. If her husband, Clarence, your grandfather, were still alive they would have been married forty-five years."

"I never knew him."

"He was a good man. A very good man. They had a good marriage until the cancer took him. He died before you were born, when your mother was still a girl."

"Will there be many people there?"

Olaf laughed. "*All* the people will be there."

Chapter Eight

Saturday came fast, too fast for the boy, but not so fast that he did not have time to think of the problems he faced.

He had never been to a party.

He did not know any of the people who would be there.

He had never been to a dance.

He could not speak to girls.

He could not be with crowds of strangers.

He could not, he finally decided, go.

The boy started in early in the day on Saturday. As they did morning chores he mentioned that he was not feeling well. His grandmother felt his head and Olaf and Gunnar both looked at him strangely.

"You did not seem sick at breakfast," Olaf said. "You ate good."

"He ate more than me," Gunnar said. "More than both of us."

"I just feel kind of sick," the boy said, knowing it was a lost cause. "It only came over me now."

"Well," his grandmother said, "I'll just have to stay home tonight and make sure you are all right."

The looks Olaf and Gunnar sent him were withering and he knew it was over. "I think it will be all right. I think I just drank too much milk. I'm still not used to whole milk."

Preparations began right after evening chores. They milked a half hour early—though Olaf said it was not good for the cows and it was difficult to get them to come into the barn early—and then went to the house and ate a light supper (just two kinds of meat, potatoes, canned peas and corn, rhubarb pie and milk and coffee) and then began the cleaning-up process.

Olaf and Gunnar took off their shirts, rehooked their bibs—still with their long underwear on—and scrubbed their heads and hands at the kitchen sink until they looked raw. Then they went into their rooms and put on clean bib overalls and clean work shirts, buttoned up tight to the collar.

The boy wore clean jeans and tennis shoes and a clean work shirt his grandmother had bought for him before he came. He tucked the shirt into his jeans but felt decidedly misdressed. In those days in the city it was thought cool to wear engineer boots with a strap and buckle, and jeans down low with the belt loops cut out of them, and a leather jacket or a T-shirt with a cigarette pack rolled up in the sleeve and to have a ducktail haircut or at least a flattop. It was *not* cool to have scraggly hair that needed cutting but was not long enough for a proper ducktail, and to wear tennis shoes and jeans with a belt and a blue work shirt tucked in, and he once again wished he were not going but knew there was no way around it.

His grandmother had a room upstairs and she came down in a new dress with light red flowers all over it, with her hair in a bun and a new kind of hairpin holding it back and up that looked like a pearl comb.

"You look like spring," Olaf said, smiling. "Like early summer is coming."

Gunnar smiled. "If you keep this up I will have to do another carving."

She blushed and waved them away. "You talk silly now," she said. "It's just a dress."

"With a new pattern *and* a new hairpin, I think . . ." Olaf laughed.

But his grandmother walked through the kitchen and out before he could say more. The men followed her out and Gunnar started the truck. His grandmother climbed into the middle and Gunnar drove and Olaf rode on the right. The boy sat in back and they moved through the evening dusk, seven miles at thirty miles an hour, until they came to Grant.

It was not a proper town. There was a small hut for a post office, a beer hall, a store that was closed and a frame building painted white that served as a community center, voting place, dance hall and sometimes church.

There was electricity in Grant, but just. There were no streetlights or outside lights except for a bulb over the door of the store and another over the entry to the dance hall. These were bare bulbs, not over a hundred watts, and yet they still brought in what looked like every bug in the county. The bulb over the dance-hall door was so surrounded by moths that the light seemed to be a dim glow four or five feet across.

There were eight or ten old trucks parked in

the front of the dance hall on the dirt road and—this was a surprise—four wagons pulled by horses. The horses were unhooked and tied around back to a rope between two trees, standing patiently in the dark, swatting mosquitoes with their tails.

To avoid the bugs, adults did not tarry at the door but went right in. There were some younger children playing outside—six- and seven-year-olds—and they slowed and stopped and watched the boy as he went inside with his grandmother and Olaf and Gunnar, the children whispering because the boy was new and strange. Later he discovered that he was related to most of them in one way or another but he had never lived nearby so knew none of them.

Inside the dance hall there was a kind of orderly disorder. At one end of a large, open room with exposed rafters was a galvanized stock tank full of cold water and brown bottles of beer and clear bottles of homemade root beer. There were also two large galvanized Thermos containers—five gallons each—of sugared concentrated grape juice mixed with water. Along one wall was a table made of slab wood from a sawmill and on the table were bowls and plates of food: potato salad, cake, cookies, cold sausage, loaves of bread, rolls, sweets, trays of venison and fish, jugs of maple syrup, jars of honey, dozens of jars of jelly and jam . . . It seemed endless and his grandmother stopped just inside the door.

"I forgot to bring food."

"Not for us," Olaf said, pushing her gently on. "Tonight is for you and Clarence, and the guest of honor doesn't bring food. Besides, we brought the music."

Overhead hung another bare bulb, this one perhaps 150 watts—or it might have been brighter because there were not so many moths around it—and the boy could see in more detail than he'd seen outside. Near the tank at the far end of the building there was a slightly elevated platform—not over a foot high—and on the platform a man stood with an accordion hanging from a strap on his neck.

He waved at Olaf and Gunnar as they came in, and held up a bottle of beer. There was no furniture and the bare pine floor had been polished smooth by years of dancing. Around the room stood men and women, and boys and girls about the same age as the boy. There must have been forty or so altogether. The men and women stood in couples but the boys stood apart from the girls, who all seemed to be blond with blue eyes and who all suddenly seemed to be staring at the new boy.

He was immediately aware that he had the wrong clothes to be cool, though he was dressed much the same as everybody there, and that he didn't know anybody. He felt immediately and viciously shy. In an instant he was alone. Gunnar and Olaf moved up to the raised bandstand and his grandmother slid off to the side to say hello to a group of women.

He stood for a second, then saw a place in the

corner by the bandstand where nobody was standing and walked over there—sure all eyes were on him—and stood at last with his back to the wall. His mouth felt dry and he stared at the rafters in the ceiling and he thought how good a root beer or grape drink would taste but to get one he would have to leave his corner, walk out in front of the bandstand where everybody could see him and around to the stock tank and back—an impossible journey. He desperately needed something to happen, and as if in answer to a prayer Gunnar took rib bones from his pocket and rattled them to get the room's attention. Olaf took his fiddle out of the case and tuned it to the accordion and without further ado they broke into a wild schottische that filled the room. Within moments there was a line of men and women dancing around the room in a circle—one, two, three steps forward, one step back, one, two, three steps forward, one step back, all in time to the heavy beat, with the men slamming their feet hard on the steps and the women moving lightly, swinging on the arms of the men as they wheeled around the room.

Gunnar turned and motioned for the boy to get out on the floor but he would not, could not, and shook his head. Gunnar signaled to Olaf, who was fiddling with quick sweeps of the bow and did not have time to reply.

The schottische was a warm-up dance—not just for the dancers but for the three musicians—and the room soon smelled of sweat and beer and sounded with laughter. The dance lasted a full fifteen minutes, growing in volume and increasing in tempo until only the strong could keep up, and at last there were just two couples stomping and wheeling around the floor as Olaf and the violin and the accordion passed the music back and forth until, finally, Olaf broke a string and the song ended.

"I will need to put in a new string," Olaf said. "Everybody should take a short rest."

Olaf and Gunnar took root beers and Gunnar handed the boy one while Olaf attached a new piece of catgut and stretched it and turned it in small squawks.

"You did not dance," Gunnar said. "This is a dance. You are supposed to dance. Are there not enough girls for you? Find a girl and dance."

Olaf put a hand on Gunnar's arm. "It does not matter if he dances. Besides, it is time now for Alida's song. *She* will pick who is to dance."

Olaf stood and talked to the accordion player, who nodded and found a different chord on the keyboard.

"Everybody to the sides," Olaf said. "This next dance is called "Alida's Song" and it is for Alida and Clarence. Everybody knows this would be their anniversary except that Clarence is gone and so Alida can pick anybody she chooses to dance with her."

While he spoke Olaf resined his bow and when he started only the violin spoke. And it was a violin now, not a fiddle, and it spoke in low, soft music for a full half minute before the accordion came in, not as an accordion but as an organ, soft as well, the notes curving out across the floor to where Alida was standing to the side.

Olaf did not look at her but had his eyes closed and the violin spoke and the accordion followed until the boy could almost see what Clarence and Alida had been when they first met, the love they had, and then his grandmother moved, came walking down the side of the room and stood in front of him and held out her hand.

"I don't . . . I mean I can't . . ."

"Yes," she said, nodding. "You can. I taught you. Come dance with me now."

And he took her hand and she put his other hand on her waist and her hand on his shoulder and they started to dance around the floor. At first he was all feet, and so embarrassed he could hardly think, but then he started moving with the music, moving her with it and then, without thinking, he was doing it, dancing with her.

She laughed and her eyes looked young and for a second, almost two seconds, she looked like

Gunnar's carving, and like a picture he had seen that his mother had, of his grandmother when she was young, standing next to Clarence, tall and straight, the old photo tinted to show red cheeks and blond hair, Clarence serious but she with a small twinkle in her eye as if she knew some great and wonderful secret.

"You have a lot of Clarence in the way you look," she told him, "and the way you dance and laugh, and the way you hit the geese and swear."

"I didn't think you heard."

"You must learn all things," she said, "how to dance and laugh and see things and even swear. You must learn them all, but now just listen to Olaf's song for Clarence and me and let me close my eyes and dance."

And he did not think any longer but swirled her around and around and danced with her until her face shone with perspiration and she smiled and said, "It is enough, enough," and he moved her to the side and brought her a glass of grape juice and then turned to see a girl named Helen with blond hair and blue eyes and she was smiling and he took her hand as easily as if he'd been doing it all his life.

And after Helen a Betty and then a Margaret and he danced with them all, some of them two and three times, until some of the boys were mad but he didn't care. He danced until his legs ached, danced until he had laughed himself hoarse, danced until Gunnar had had one too many beers and had to crawl into the back of the truck to sleep, and he was at last riding home, Olaf driving with his grandmother between them, and he turned to her and said:

"Thank you, Grandma."

"For what?" She smiled, the moonlight showing her cheeks.

"For . . . for dancing with me . . . for helping me." He sighed. "For the best night in my whole life, thank you."

"Oh," she said, "it was not so much as that.

You will have many more nights and many more dances."

And he did. He worked all that summer and each Saturday Olaf handed him eighteen dollars and he would take the truck to town and dance and sometimes walk in the moonlight with a girl and talk of his dreams or their dreams and he fell in love, or thought he did, or wanted to think he did, with Helen, and he felt his heart would break when she moved to the Twin Cities and they swore eternal this and eternal that and he never saw her again. Never heard from her again. And he grew up and away and met other Helens and other Bettys and found larger jobs and then, finally, the army. He left the army and worked many jobs. He married and had a family. And he never knew until after his grandmother had passed on, never knew that she had planned the whole summer.

Planned it because he was in trouble with his life, and she saved him just as she had when he was five years old, when his mother was drunk and wild in Chicago during the Second World War and his grandmother took him in to live with her when she was cooking for a work crew building roads up into Canada; planned on helping him to grow, to change, to find the world and himself. Planned the job with Olaf and Gunnar. Much later, when he was older still and not much wiser he would find that Olaf and Gunnar had not needed a person to work with them on the farm, that indeed they could not have afforded it; that they lived on much less than they had paid him and that each Saturday his grandmother had handed Olaf eighteen dollars to give to the boy so that her grandson would think he was working for pay.

He found all this in a small cigar box full of letters in her basement. He came across the box after she was gone, in a letter to her sister, when he, the boy, was old enough to have grandchildren of his own, and he sat with the letters and cried and remembered the dance and the night and the summer and thought that even now, with her gone so many years, even now she was still there, still holding his hand on the dance floor, still guiding him, still helping him.